and then it's spring

Julie Fogliano

ILLUSTRATED BY
Erin E. Stead

SCHOLASTIC INC.

First you have brown,
all around you have brown

then there are seeds

and a wish for rain,

and then it rains

and it is still brown,
but a hopeful, very possible sort of brown,

an *is that a little green?*

no, it's just brown sort of brown

then it is a week

and you worry
about those little seeds

and if maybe it was the birds,

or maybe it was the bears and all that stomping,
because bears can't read signs
that say things like
"please do not stomp here—
there are seeds
and they are trying"

and then it is one more week,

and the brown,
still brown,
has a greenish hum
that you can only hear
if you put your ear to the ground
and close your eyes

and then it is one more week

and a sunny day,
that sunny day that happens
right after that rainy day

and you walk outside
to check on all that brown,

but the brown isn't around
and now you have green,
all around
you have
green.

please do not
stomp here
there are seeds and they are trying

for enzo, nico, and josh,
who love to go outside and notice things
—j.f.
for julie, josh, george, jason,
jennifer, nick, patty, and sara
—e.s.

ISBN 978-0-545-55106-9

Text copyright © 2012 by Julie Fogliano.
Illustrations copyright © 2012 by Erin E. Stead.
All rights reserved. Published by Scholastic Inc.,
557 Broadway, New York, NY 10012,
by arrangement with Roaring Brook Press, a division of
Holtzbrinck Publishing Holdings Limited Partnership.
SCHOLASTIC and associated logos are trademarks
and/or registered trademarks of Scholastic Inc.

12 11 10 9 8 7 6 5 4 3 2 1   13 14 15 16 17 18/0

Printed in the U.S.A.   40

First Scholastic printing, January 2013

Book design by Philip C. Stead and Jennifer Browne